For Mr. Bean and his wonderful hairy coat.
H. L. Goldsworthy

For Ben Hooley, who grew a very long beard for the Rockinghorse appeal.
Georgie Birkett

First American edition published in 2008 by Boxer Books Limited.

Distributed in the United States and Canada by Sterling Publishing Co., Inc.
387 Park Avenue South, New York, NY 10016-8810

First published in Great Britain in 2008 by Boxer Books Limited.
www.boxerbooks.com

Library of Congress Cataloging-in-Publication Data available.

ISBN 13: 978-1-906250-10-2

1 3 5 7 9 10 8 6 4 2

Printed in China

All of our papers are sourced from managed forests and renewable resources.

Mr. Follycule's
Wonderful Beard

Written by H. L. Goldsworthy

Illustrated by Georgie Birkett

Boxer Books

Mr. Follycule had no hair.

Not a single strand!
He was as bald as a beach ball!

One night Mr. Follycule looked in the mirror and said,

"I wish I had some hair and a wonderful beard to take care of."

The next morning, Mr. Follycule looked

in the mirror and got a big surprise.

His head was as bald as ever.

But his chin was covered with bristles.

He inspected his stubble very closely.

He looked at it front-ways . . .

and sideways . . .

Stubble!
I have stubble!

He looked at it close up
through a magnifying glass.
He even tried to creep up on it
in the mirror to make sure the
stubble was still there.

Mr. Follycule went to work a very very happy man.

But Mr. Follycule's boss, Mr. Thiswontdo, saw the stubble and said, in a rather loud voice, "Mr. Follycule! You are a disgrace to this office. Tomorrow, do not have that messy stubble on your face!"

Now Mr. Follycule felt sad. That night he shaved his lovely, bristly stubble and went to bed with a smooth, soft chin once again.

The next morning, Mr. Follycule's stubble was back.

But this time it was longer and stronger.

Quickly, Mr. Follycule shaved. But no sooner had

he finished shaving than the stubble grew back—

even longer, stronger, and thicker!

The stubble was growing into a big, bushy beard.

Mr. Follycule's wonderful new beard was furry
and fuzzy and shaggy and very, very, very hairy!
He brushed his new beard very gently and felt very proud.
And he walked to work feeling very happy.

On the way, Mr. Follycule heard
two boys whispering about his beard.

The beard had not stopped growing.

It was growing faster and faster;
furrier, fuzzier, shaggier—and
even more hairy!

At the office, everyone laughed out loud—except Mr. Thiswontdo, who said,

"That beard looks ridiculous!"

This quite upset Mr. Follycule—so much so that he ate his lunch by himself in the park.

It was a very cold day. A shivery day.

But Mr. Follycule had his nice long beard to keep him warm—a beard that kept growing and growing.

Overnight, Mr. Follycule's beard
grew even more—
wider than his bed,
longer than a bus,
bushier than a big, bushy bear.

It grew out his bedroom door,
down the stairs, and curled
around his comfy chair.

But it didn't stop there . . . .

Oh, no! It had grown out the window, across the lawn, and under the cars in the street. It had grown around the street lights and was blocking traffic. Some people laughed, but many people looked angry. Moms, dads, aunties, uncles, grannies and granddads, babies, children and teenagers all pointed at Mr. Follycule's extraordinary beard.

And poor Mr. Follycule
was very embarrassed.

Mr. Follycule took a pair of scissors and cut off his beautiful beard.

It took him all day to clean up the hair. He piled it into one hundred big sacks, put them away in his garage, and went to bed. He was so tired.

That night it snowed.

It snowed all night.

It snowed all day.

It snowed and snowed
and snowed—
for a whole week.

Mr. Follycule couldn't get to work.

Nobody could get to work.

Then Mr. Follycule had an idea.

He took the bags of his beard, washed it all, and started knitting.

He knitted all day.
He knitted all night.
He knitted and knitted and knitted.

Late in the evening,
Mr. Follycule put all
his knitted things
back into the sacks.

Then he went from door
to door and left presents
for all his neighbors.

Each package had
a little note saying:
"Sorry!"

When Mr. Follycule was finished,
he went home, brushed his little beard,
and went to bed.

Mr. Follycule woke up to the sound of people

calling his name. He hurried outside.

His beard had stopped growing.

The snow had stopped snowing.

His lawn was full of happy, smiling people—

all wearing and using his

extraordinary knitted gifts.

And there was the biggest snowman

Mr. Follycule had ever seen.

It was holding a huge sign that said:

"Three cheers for Mr. Follycule and

his wonderful beard!"